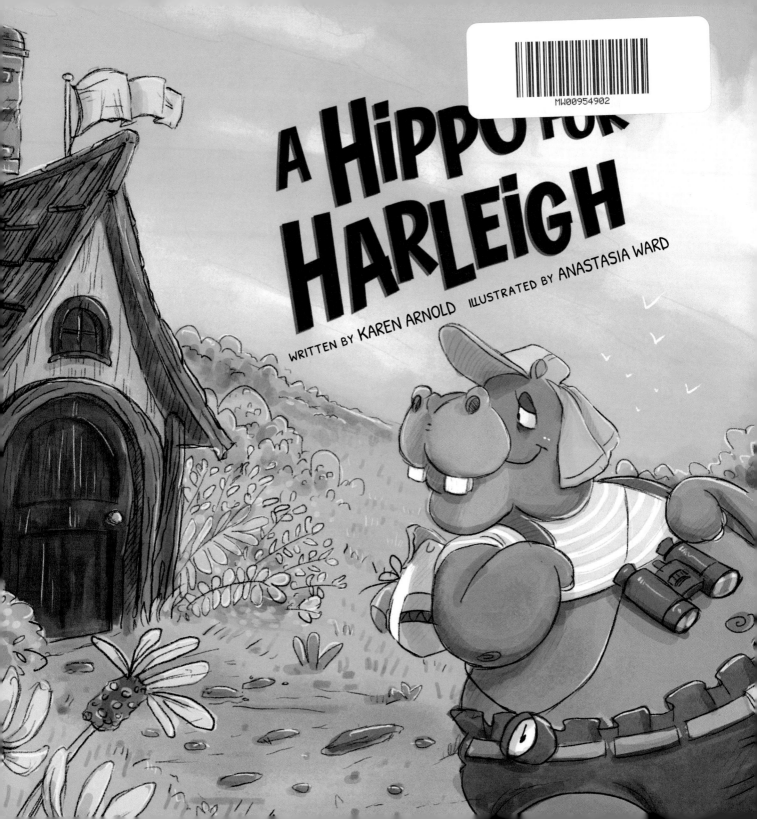

A HiPPO for HARLEIGH

WRITTEN BY KAREN ARNOLD   ILLUSTRATED BY ANASTASIA WARD

For Dr. Harbir Makin, an honest healer and humble humanitarian.

First paperback edition September 2020

Book illustrations and design by Anastasia Ward Illustrations
AnastasiaWardIllustrations.com

Edited by Jena Benton Lasley
JenaBenton.com

ISBN 9798678888310
Library of Congress Control Number: 2020916912

Published by PeachesPublishing

It was a hectic day at Harleigh's Hospital.

Hazel the Honeybee was trying to fly home,
but her wing had not healed.

Henry the Hyena couldn't stop laughing
and he had the hiccups.

And Helen the Horse,
who was hobbling around on crutches,
was trying to hold onto her new handbag,
but it kept falling on the floor.

Harleigh wanted them all to be healthy,
but she only had two hands.
"How will I handle one more patient?"
Harleigh thought to herself.

"You look like you need a break, Harleigh," exclaimed her friends, Hamster and Hedgehog.

"We think you should go out for a hike! We'll hang out here and help."

"Perhaps you're right," said Harleigh.
"I'll get my hat."

So Harleigh began hiking up a hill near her home.

She hiked higher...

... and higher.

It was very hot outside and
her backpack was getting heavy.

"Maybe it's time I hurry back."
Harleigh thought to herself.

Then all of a sudden she came to a halt!

She could hardly believe her eyes!
There was a huge hippo sitting under a large hollow tree!
He was holding his head and he seemed very unhappy.

"Hello! My name's Harleigh.
Are you hurt?"

"Yes," replied the hippo.
"My name's Hector.
I hit my head on that branch
and I'm very hungry."

"Well I think I can help you, Hector.
Will you come home with me to my hospital?"

"HOSPITAL?!" exclaimed Hector.
"I'm afraid of hospitals."

"Oh it's a very nice place, Hector.
I can give you some ice for your headache
and a delicious homemade snack to eat."
"Oh, I don't know." said Hector.
"I promise to take good care of you," assured Harleigh. "Here, hold my hand."

So Harleigh and Hector
carefully made their way down the hill.
When they arrived at the hospital,
Hamster and Hedgehog greeted them happily.
They even gave Hector a great big hug!

"Wait here, Hector.
I'll be back with some ice and a snack."
comforted Harleigh.

Hector hoped she would hurry
... and she did.

"Here. Put this on your head where it hurts.
Then you can enjoy these delicious hazelnuts."

"Umm, no thank you." said Hector.

So Harleigh handed him
some juicy huckleberries right off the bush.

"No thank you."

"Hold on, Hector.
I think I have just the thing!"

Harleigh asked Helen the Horse
if she would mind sharing some of her hay.

"No thank you." sighed Hector.
He was getting hungrier and hungrier.

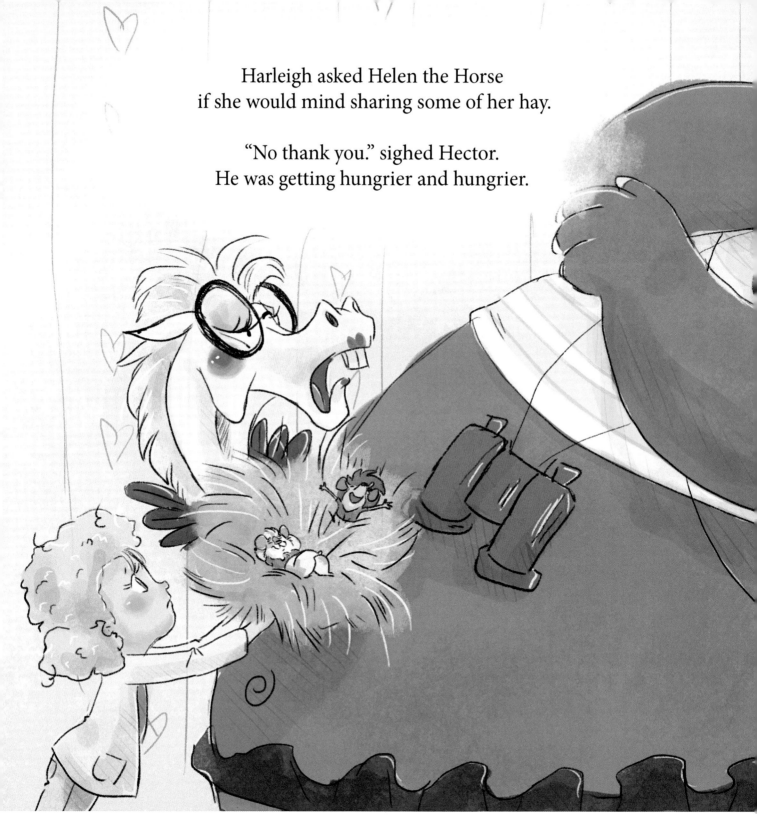

"Oh, Hector. I feel horrible. I promised
I would take good care of you and I haven't.
I'm afraid I only have hotdogs and hamburgers
left to offer you."

"Hotdogs and hamburgers?!" exclaimed Hector.

"Yes," said Harleigh, helplessly.
"I know hippos don't like hotdogs and hamburgers."

"Really?" said Hector.
"I guess they don't know what they're missing!
Hotdogs and hamburgers are *my* favorite!"

"HURRAY!" shouted the animals.
"Happy day!" cried Harleigh.

That evening, Henry the Hyena played the harmonica.
Hamster and Hedgehog danced the Hokey Pokey.
Hector, however, just sat quietly.
He was enjoying eating hotdogs and hamburgers
in perfect harmony at Harleigh's Hospital.
And guess what?

He wasn't scared at all.